Going to the Doctor

PaRragon

Bath • New York • Singapore • Hong Kong • Cologne • Delhi
Melbourne • Amsterdam • Johannesburg • Auckland • Shenzhen

Page 7

Pages 10-11

Page 11

Page 12

Page 15

Page 16

Page 17

Page 18

Page 21

Page 23

Page 29

How to Use This Book

 Read the story, all about Joshua and Isabella's trip to the doctor.

 Look closely at each picture in the story. You may be asked to find or count things in a scene and place a sticker on the page.

 Try each activity as you go along, or read the story first, then go back and do the activities. The answers are at the bottom of each activity page.

 Some pictures will need stickers to finish the scenes or activities. Any leftover stickers can be used to decorate the book or your things.

Joshua doesn't feel well.
He has a stuffy nose and a sore throat.
Joshua's mom is taking him to see the doctor.

Find these things outside the doctors' office.

Joshua's friend Isabella is going with them.
She had a tummy ache but she now feels better
and needs a check-up too.

Count the number of birds in the picture.

Doctors' office

Put your butterfly sticker here.

Joshua hasn't been to the doctor for a long time. He's not sure what will happen there.

"Don't worry," Isabella tells him. "Dr. Hope is really nice. She helped me feel better, and she will help you feel better, too."

While the friends are waiting, Isabella shows Joshua a toy doctor kit.

Reception

Can you find these things in the waiting room?

It has a pretend stethoscope and a little flashlight for looking in your ears. "Dr. Hope has real ones just like these," she tells Joshua.

Find the stickers to finish the picture.

Find the sticker of Joshua.

11

Joshua finds a box of toys in the waiting room.
He and Isabella build a castle.

Find the stickers to finish the picture.

Count the red blocks in the castle.
How many blue ones?
What other colors are there?

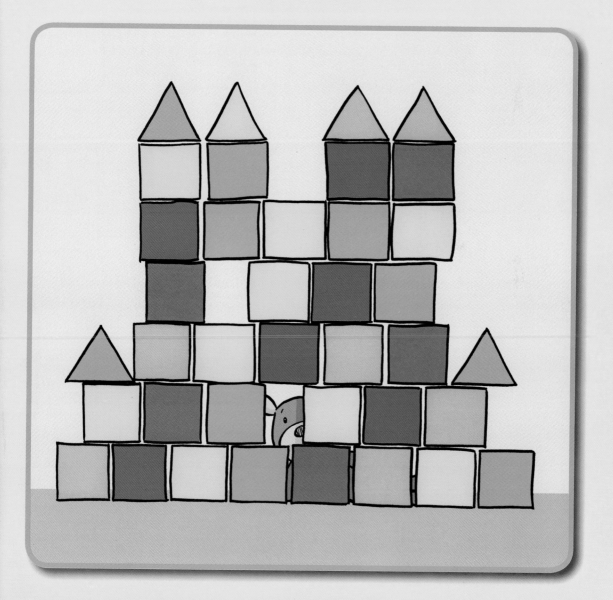

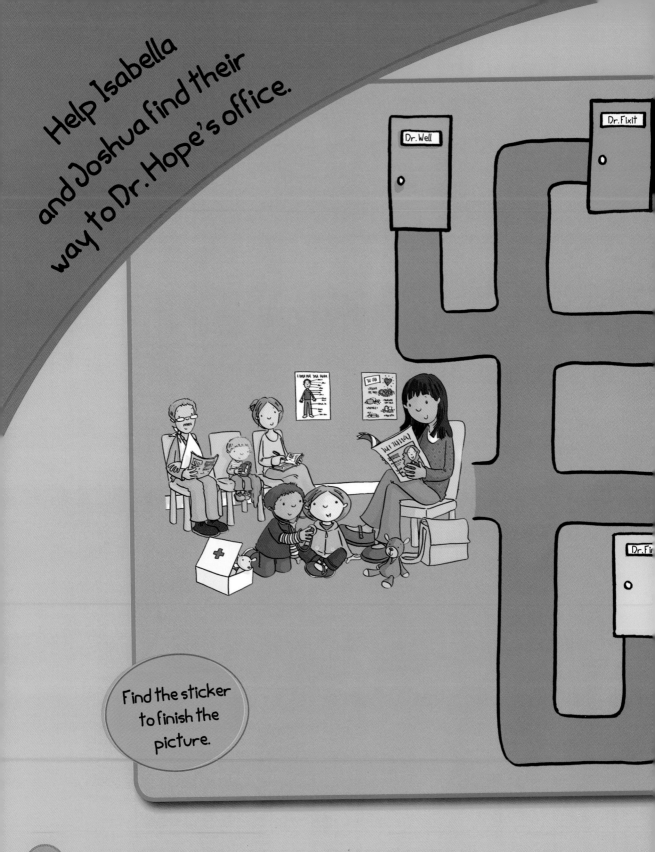

Help Isabella and Joshua find their way to Dr. Hope's office.

Find the sticker to finish the picture.

Dr. Good

Answer

Dr. Hope calls Joshua and Isabella into her office. She does Isabella's checkup first. Dr. Hope checks Isabella's weight and height.

Find the sticker to finish the picture.

Find these things in Dr. Hope's office.

Then she gently checks Isabella's tummy.
"Hee-hee," Isabella giggles. "That tickles!"
"Everything is just fine," says Dr. Hope.

Put your teddy bear sticker here.

It's Joshua's turn now. He tells Dr. Hope about his scratchy throat and stuffy nose. She takes his temperature. "No fever," she says. "That's good!"

Find the stickers to finish the picture.

Can you find five differences between these two pictures?

Answer

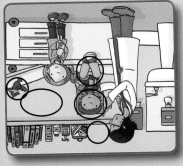

Dr. Hope listens to Joshua's heart and breathing with her stethoscope. It's just like the one in the toy doctor kit!

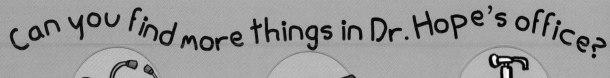
Can you find more things in Dr. Hope's office?

"Nice and strong," says Dr. Hope. She looks in Joshua's ears with her special little flashlight. "It's just like the toy flashlight," says Isabella.

Put your box of band-aids sticker here.

Which of these things would you find at the doctor's office?

Answer

Dr. Hope looks at Joshua's throat.
"Say 'Aaaah,'" she says, and Joshua does.
"Good job!" says Dr. Hope.

Find the stickers to finish the picture.

Can you find these things in the picture opposite?

Answer

"You have a throat infection," Dr. Hope tells Joshua. "That's why you don't feel well."

"But there is a medicine that will make you feel better very soon," Dr. Hope continued. "Your mom can get it from the drugstore."

"You have both been very brave today,"
Dr. Hope tells Isabella and Joshua.
"Would you each like to choose a sticker?"

Isabella chooses the pink sticker.
Joshua likes the blue one.

Do you know your
shapes and colors?
How many circles are there?
What colors can you see?

At home, Mom gives Joshua some of the medicine Dr. Hope prescribed.

Find these things in the kitchen.

"It tastes like bananas!" Joshua says.
Then he and Isabella go to Joshua's room to play.

Put your dog sticker here.

"I feel better already," Joshua tells Isabella. "I'm really happy I went to the doctor, and I'm happy you were there with me!"